Grandma's Doll

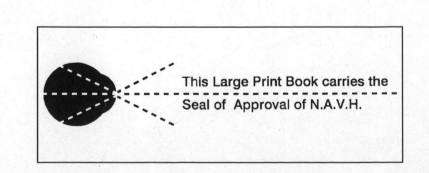

This Large Print Book carries the
Seal of Approval of N.A.V.H.

GRANDMA'S DOLL

WANDA E. BRUNSTETTER

THORNDIKE PRESS

A part of Gale, Cengage Learning

GALE
CENGAGE Learning·

Detroit • New York • San Francisco • New Haven, Conn • Waterville, Maine • London

GALE
CENGAGE Learning®

LIBRARY OF CONGRESS CATALOGING-IN-PUBLICATION DATA

Brunstetter, Wanda E.
    Grandma's doll / by Wanda E. Brunstetter. — Large print ed.
      p. cm. — (Thorndike Press large print Christian romance)
    (Love finds a Way; #2)
    ISBN 978-1-4104-4757-9 (alk. paper) — ISBN 1-4104-4757-X (alk. paper)
    1. Young women—Fiction. 2. Widowers—Fiction. 3. Cooks—Fiction.
    4. Antique dealers—Fiction. 5. Fathers and daughters—Fiction. 6. Large
    type books. I. Title.
    PS3602.R864G73 2012
    813'.6—dc23   2012006690

Published in 2012 by arrangement with Barbour Publishing, Inc.

Printed in the United States of America
4 5 6 7 16 15 14 13 12

In loving memory of my
Aunt Margaret, who gave me her
Bye-Lo baby doll many years ago.
Thank you for the special treasure
I will someday give to one of my
granddaughters.

CHAPTER 1

Sheila Nickels shivered as a blast of chilly March air pushed against her body. She slipped the tarnished key into the lock and opened the door. This was Grandma's house — the place where Sheila had come throughout her childhood for holidays, special occasions, and everything in between. She'd felt warmth, love, and joy whenever she visited this Victorian home on the north side of Casper, Wyoming.

Sheila stepped into the dark entryway and felt for the light switch on the wall closest to the door. "At least the electricity hasn't been turned off yet," she murmured.

An eerie sense of aloneness settled over her as she moved to the living room. Everything looked so strange. Much of Grandma's furniture was missing, and the pieces left had been draped with white sheets, including the upright piano Sheila and her cousins used to plunk on. Several cardboard boxes sat in one corner of the room, waiting to be hauled away. It was a dreary sight.

A sigh stuck in Sheila's throat, and she swallowed it down. She'd just come from visiting her grandmother at Mountain Springs Retirement Center on the other side of town. Grandma's one-bedroom apartment looked like a fishbowl compared to this grand home where Grandma and Grandpa Dunmore had lived for over fifty years. Grandpa passed away two years ago, but Grandma had continued to stay here until she finally decided taking care of the house was too much for her. She'd moved to the retirement center a few weeks ago.

Grandma's old house didn't look the same without the clutter of her antique furniture. It didn't sound the same without Grandma's cheerful voice calling from the kitchen, "Girls, come have some chocolate chip cookies and a glass of milk."

Sheila slipped off her coat and draped it across the arm of an overstuffed chair. She then placed her purse on the oak end table and turned toward the stairs. She was here at her grandmother's request and needed to follow through with what she'd set out to do.

As a feeling of nostalgia washed over her, Sheila climbed the steps leading to the second floor. Another flight of stairs took her to the attic, filled with so many wonderful treasures. A chain dangled from the light fixture overhead, and Sheila gave it a yank.

"Kimber, Lauren, Jessica, and I used to play here," she whispered into the dusty, unfinished room. She lowered herself to the lid of an antique trunk and closed her eyes, allowing the memories of days gone by to wash over her.

"Look at me, Sheila. Aren't I beautiful?"

Sheila giggled as her cousin Lauren pranced in front of her wearing a pair of black patent leather heels that were much too big for her seven-year-old feet. Wrapped in a multicolored crocheted shawl with a crazy-looking green hat on her head, Lauren continued to swagger back and forth.

"You can play dress-up if you want to, but I'm gonna get the Bye-Lo baby and take her for a ride." Sheila scrambled over to the wicker carriage, where the bisque-headed doll was nestled beneath a tiny patchwork quilt. Grandma had told her she'd made the covering many years ago when she was a little girl.

Of all the treasures in her grandmother's attic, the Bye-Lo baby was Sheila's favorite. She could play with it for hours while her three girl cousins found other things to do.

Sheila leaned over and scooped the precious doll into her arms. "Bye-Lo, I wish you could be mine forever."

Sheila's eyes snapped open as she returned to the present. Since Grandma had already moved, her house would soon be put up for sale. She'd called Sheila at her home in Fresno, California, and invited her to choose something from the attic that was special to her. Sheila knew right away what that *something* would be — the Bye-Lo baby doll. Some might think it was silly, but when she was a child, Sheila had prayed she could own the doll someday, and her prayers were finally being answered. Now all she had to do was find her treasure.

Sheila scanned the perimeter of the attic. An old dresser sat near the trunk, and an intricately designed wooden container was a few feet away. Her gaze came to rest on the small wicker doll carriage, which Bye-Lo used to lie in. It was empty.

"How odd. The doll always sat in that baby carriage." She stood and lifted the lid of the trunk. "Maybe it's in here."

Near the bottom she found several pieces of clothing that had belonged to the doll. There was even a photograph of young

Sheila holding her favorite attic treasure. The dolls she had owned as a child hadn't been nearly as special as Bye-Lo. The church her father had pastored then was small and didn't pay much. Sheila had learned early in life to accept secondhand items and be grateful, but she'd always wished for more.

She grabbed the picture and placed it in the pocket of her blue jeans, then slammed the trunk lid. "That doll has to be in this house someplace, and I'm not leaving until I find it!"

The telephone jingled, and Dwaine Woods picked it up on the second ring. "The Older the Better," he said into the receiver. "May I help you?"

"Is Bill Summers there?" a woman's gravelly voice questioned.

"Sorry, but Bill's not here. He sold his business to me a few months ago."

"Oh, I see. Well, this is Lydia Dunmore, and I did some business with The Older the Better Antique Shop when Bill owned it."

"Is there something I can help you with, Ms. Dunmore?" Dwaine asked.

"As a matter of fact, there is. I'd like to see about having my old piano appraised. I've recently moved and will need to sell it."

"Sure. No problem. When would you like to have the appraisal done?"

"How about this afternoon? One of my granddaughters is at the house right now, and she could let you in."

Dwaine reached for a notepad and pen. "If you'll give me the address, I'll run over there and take a look. Would you like me to call you with my estimate, or should I give it to your granddaughter?"

"Just give it to Sheila. She'll be coming back to the retirement center where I live to return my house key sometime before she leaves Casper."

Dwaine wrote down the particulars, and a few minutes later he hung up the phone. Lydia Dunmore's house was on the other side of town, but he could be there in ten minutes. He put the CLOSED sign in the store's front window, grabbed his jacket off the antique coat tree, and headed out the door. Things had been slow at The Older the Better this week, but it looked like business might be picking up.

With an exasperated groan, Sheila shut the lid on the cedar chest — the last place she had searched for Grandma's old doll. For the past couple of hours, she'd looked through countless boxes and trunks, organizing each one as she went. Except for the room being much cleaner now, her trip to the attic had been fruitless. There was no doll to be found.

"Grandma would probably tell me to choose something else," Sheila muttered, "but nothing here matters to me except the Bye-Lo baby."

Once more, Sheila thought about her grandmother's recent move and consoled herself with the fact that if Grandma hadn't left this rambling old house, Sheila and her girl cousins wouldn't have been asked to choose something special from the attic. The boy cousins had been invited to check out the basement for an item they would like to have.

"Too bad I can't find what's special to me," she grumbled.

Maybe the doll had been removed from the attic and was in one of the boxes downstairs. Sheila decided it was worth the time to take a look. She yanked on the chain to turn off the light and headed for the stairs. If she didn't find Bye-Lo in the next hour or so, she planned to head back to the retirement center. Maybe Grandma could shed some light on the doll's disappearance.

Sheila entered the living room and was about to kneel in front of a cardboard box when the doorbell rang. "I wonder who that could be."

She went to the front door and looked through the peephole. A man stood on the porch — an attractive man with sandy-blond hair and brown eyes. Sheila didn't recognize him, but then she hadn't lived in Casper for twelve years and didn't get back for visits very often. The man could be one of Grandma's neighbors for all she knew. He could even be a salesman, a Realtor, or . . .

The bell rang again, and Sheila jumped. Should she open the door? She sent up a quick prayer. *Protect me, Lord, if this man's a criminal.*

She slipped the security chain in place and opened the door the few inches it would go. "May I help you?"

"Hi, I'm Dwaine Woods from The Older the Better Antique Shop across town. I got a call to come here and take a look at an old piano."

Sheila's gaze darted to the living room. Grandma obviously had left the piano behind because there wasn't enough room in her apartment at the retirement center. How sad that Grandma felt forced to sell something she'd dearly loved for so many years.

"I have my business card right here if you'd like to see it," Dwaine said, as if sensing her reservations about opening the door. He reached into his jacket pocket, pulled out a leather wallet, and withdrew a card. "I bought the place from Bill Summers not long ago." He slipped it through the small opening, and Sheila clasped the card between her thumb and index finger. She studied it a few seconds and decided it looked legitimate.

"Who asked you to look at the piano?" she asked with hesitation.

"Lydia Dunmore. She called awhile ago and said she'd like an estimate. Told me her granddaughter Sheila was here and would let me in." He shuffled his feet across the wooden planks on the porch. "I presume that would be you?"

Sheila opened her mouth to reply, but the sharp ringing of the telephone halted her words. "I'd better get that. Be right back." She shut the door before Dwaine had a chance to say anything more.

Not knowing how long he might be expected to wait, Dwaine flopped into the wicker chair near the door. He couldn't believe how nervous the young woman seemed. She acted like she didn't believe

Lydia Dunmore had called and asked him to give an estimate on the piano.

She must not be from around here. Most everyone I know is pretty trusting. Dwaine hadn't been able to get a good look at her face through the small opening in the doorway, but he had seen her eyes. They were blue, like a cloudless sky, and they'd revealed obvious fear.

Sure hope she comes back soon and lets me in. Now that the sun's going down, it's getting cold out here. Dwaine stuffed his hands inside his jacket pockets while he tapped his foot impatiently. Finally, he heard the door creak open. A young woman with jet-black hair curling around her face in soft waves stared at him.

"Sorry for making you wait so long," she said. "That was my grandmother on the phone. She called to let me know you were coming to look at the piano."

Dwaine stood. "Does that mean I can come in?"

She nodded, and her cheeks turned pink as a sunset. "I'm Sheila Nickels."

Dwaine stuck out his hand and was relieved when she shook it. Maybe now that her grandmother had confirmed the reason for his visit, Sheila wouldn't be so wary.

"It's nice to meet you. I take it you're not

from around here?"

She motioned him to follow as she led the way to the living room. "I grew up in Casper, but twelve years ago my folks moved to Fresno, California. My father's a minister and was offered a job at a church there. I was fourteen at the time."

"So you're a Christian, then?"

She smiled. "I have been since I was twelve and went to Bible camp. That's when I acknowledged my sins and accepted Christ as my personal Savior."

Dwaine grinned back at her. "I'm a Christian, too, and it's always nice to meet others who have put their faith in the Lord."

She nodded. "I agree."

"What brings you to this part of the country?" he asked.

Sheila motioned to the array of boxes stacked in one corner of the room. "Grandma recently moved to Mountain Springs Retirement Center, and she'll be putting this old house on the market soon."

"Which is why she wants to sell the piano?"

"Right. Grandma called me a few weeks ago and asked that I come here. She said she'd like me to choose an item from the attic — something I felt was special. Since she needed it done before the house sold, I decided to take a week's vacation and fly here before everything's been gone through." Sheila sucked in her lower lip. "She asked each of her granddaughters to come, and I'm the first to arrive."

"Have you found what you wanted yet?" he questioned.

She shook her head. "It's an old doll I'm looking for, but there was no sign of it in the attic."

Dwaine massaged the bridge of his nose. "Hmm . . . did you ask your grandmother about it? Maybe she moved the doll to some other part of the house."

Sheila pulled out the wooden piano bench and sat down. "I would have asked her when we were on the phone a few minutes ago, but I didn't want to leave you on the porch in the cold."

"If you'd like to call her back, you two can talk about the missing doll while I take a look at this old relic," he said, motioning to the piano. "I should have an estimate by the time you get off the phone."

"That sounds fine." Sheila turned and walked out of the room.

Dwaine moved over to uncover the piano and smiled. *She's sure cute. Guess I'll have to wait till she comes back to find out if she's married or not.*

CHAPTER 2

Sheila returned to the living room ten minutes later, a feeling of defeat threatening to weigh her down. She'd come all the way to Casper for nothing.

She tossed aside the white sheet on the aging, olive green sofa and groaned. "I can't believe it!"

Dwaine sat on the piano bench, writing something on a notepad, but he looked up when she made her comment. "Bad news?"

She nodded, not trusting her voice and afraid she might break into tears if she related her conversation with Grandma.

Dwaine's forehead wrinkled. "What'd your grandmother say about the doll?"

"It's gone." She paused and drew in a deep breath. "Grandma said she sold it to you."

He shook his head. "I've never met Lydia Dunmore. The first contact I've had with her was today, when she asked me to appraise this." He motioned toward the piano with his elbow.

"She said she took the Bye-Lo doll to The Older the Better Antique Shop last fall and sold it."

"That may be, but I wasn't the owner back then. I bought the place from Bill Summers two months ago."

Sheila sniffed. "Guess I'd better talk to him then. Do you have his home phone number or address?"

Dwaine fingered the small dimple in the middle of his chin. That, along with his sandy-blond hair and dark brown eyes, made him the most attractive man Sheila had met in a long time. *Of course, looks aren't everything,* she reminded herself. *Kevin Carlson was good-looking, too, and he broke my heart.*

"Bill moved to Canada right after he sold the store. I'm sorry to tell you this, but he's in the early stages of Alzheimer's, so his daughter and son-in-law came to Casper and moved him up there to be near them."

Sheila tapped her fingernails along the edge of the couch. "Are you saying he probably wouldn't remember what became of my grandmother's doll, even if I could contact him?"

"Exactly. The poor man wouldn't have

been able to handle the details of selling the store if his family hadn't taken over and done all the paperwork." Dwaine shook his head. "It's sad to see an older person forced to give everything up when some unexpected illness overtakes his body or mind."

Sheila nodded and swallowed around the lump in her throat, feeling sad for Bill Summers and thankful Grandma was still fairly healthy. Then her thoughts went to the doll she would never have, and unable to control her emotions, she covered her face and let the tears flow.

Dwaine stayed on the piano bench a few seconds, unsure of what to say or do. He didn't want Sheila to misread his intentions if he offered comfort. He wrestled with his thoughts a moment longer and finally realized he couldn't remain seated and do nothing but watch her cry.

He hurried across the room and took a seat beside her on the couch. "Would you like me to call someone — your husband, grandmother, or some other relative?"

"I–I'm not married," she said with a sniffle. "And I don't want to bother Grandma. She's got enough problems of her own right now." Sheila lifted her head and looked at him through dark, heavy lashes. Her blue eyes were luminous behind the tears that filled them, and her chin trembled as she made a feeble attempt at smiling. "Sorry for blubbering like that. I don't know what came over me."

"I'm not married either, and I may not know a lot about women, but I do have a sister who can get pretty emotional at times, so I try to be understanding when someone's in tears."

When Sheila offered him another half smile, Dwaine fought the urge to wipe away the remaining moisture on her cheeks. He couldn't explain the reason this dark-haired beauty made him feel protective. He'd just met the woman, so it made no sense at all.

"I'd like to help you find that doll," Dwaine announced.

Her eyes brightened some. "How?"

"The first place I want to look is my antique shop. Even though I haven't seen any Bye-Lo dolls lying around, she could still be there hidden away in some drawer, a box, or a closet."

Sheila's dark eyebrows disappeared under her curly bangs. "You think so?"

"It's worth checking. At the very least we ought to find a receipt showing the doll was brought into the shop, and if it was sold again, there should be a receipt for that, too." Dwaine returned to the piano bench, where he retrieved the notepad. He ripped off the top page, moved back to the sofa, and handed the paper to Sheila. "Here's the estimate on the piano. If you want to give me the phone number of the place where you're staying, I'll call you if and when I locate the doll."

She frowned. "I was hoping, before I return Grandma's house key, that I might go over to your shop and see what you can find out."

"I haven't been all that busy today, so I guess we could head over there now and take a look."

"I'd appreciate that." Sheila reached into her jeans pocket and withdrew a picture. "This is me as a child, holding the Bye-Lo, in case you're wondering what the doll looks like."

He nodded. "Yep. About the same as the ones I've seen advertised in doll collectors' magazines."

"I'm only here on a week's vacation, which means I won't be in Casper long. So if we could go to your shop now, that would be great."

It was obvious that Sheila was desperate to find her grandmother's doll, and Dwaine didn't have the heart to tell her it could take days or even weeks to go through everything in his store. Bill Summers hadn't been much of an organizer, not to mention the fact that he'd become forgetful toward the end. Dwaine had already discovered this was the reason so many things seemed to be missing or were found in some obscure places. Of course, Dwaine couldn't say much about being disorganized. Tidiness was not his best trait either.

"If you have your own car, you can follow me over to the shop. If not, I'll be happy to give you a lift," he offered.

"That won't be necessary. My rental's parked in the driveway."

"Sounds good. Are you ready to head out then?"

She nodded and grabbed her jacket from the arm of an overstuffed chair, then reached for her purse on the end table.

"Oh, and by the way," he said, turning back to the piano and lifting the sheet off the top, "I found this while I was doing my appraisal. It looks old, and I figured it might be a family treasure." He handed her a black Bible with frayed edges and several pages ready to fall out.

Sheila smiled. "Thanks. This must belong to Grandma. I'll take it to her when I return the house key. She probably didn't realize she left it on top of the piano."

Dwaine felt a sense of relief. At least Sheila was smiling again.

Sheila had never been inside an antique store so full of clutter, but she remembered Dwaine saying the previous owner's memory had been fading. The poor man probably had struggled with keeping the shop going and hadn't been able to clean or organize things. For all she knew, Dwaine might not be any better at putting the place in order. He did seem to be kind and caring though, if one could tell anything from first impressions.

Kind, caring, and cute, Sheila mused as she followed Dwaine to a long wooden counter in the center of the store. An antique cash register sat on one end, and a cordless phone was beside it. An odd contrast, to be sure.

"I'll start by looking through the receipt box," Dwaine said as he reached under the counter and retrieved a battered shoe box that looked like it belonged in the garbage.

Sheila stifled a groan. *That's where he keeps his receipts? I'd say this man's in need of a good secretary as well as some new office supplies.*

While Dwaine riffled through the papers,

Sheila leaned against the front of the counter and reflected on her job back in Fresno. For the last two years, she'd worked as a receptionist in a chiropractor's office. The clinic had been in total disarray when she was hired, and it had taken nearly six months to get everything organized. She'd finally succeeded, and the office was running more smoothly and efficiently than ever before. Dr. Taylor often praised Sheila for her organizational skills.

"Do you miss living in Wyoming, or are you a bona fide California girl now?" Dwaine asked, breaking into Sheila's thoughts.

"I like my job working as a receptionist for a chiropractor," she replied, "but I miss some things about living here."

"Such as?"

"Grandma for one. I used to love going over to her house and playing in the attic with my girl cousins. There were so many wonderful treasures there." She wrinkled her nose. "The boy cousins preferred to play outside or in the basement where they could get dirty and look for creepy crawlers."

Dwaine chuckled. "Anything else you miss about living in Casper?"

"The cold, snowy winters, when we went sledding and ice-skating."

"Guess you don't get much snow in California, huh?"

"Not in Fresno."

Dwaine laid the stack of receipts he'd already gone through on the countertop. "Is Lydia Dunmore your only relative living here now?"

"My cousin Jessica is still in the area, and so is Aunt Marlene. Mom and Dad are missionaries in Brazil, my brother lives in San Diego, and the rest of my aunts, uncles, and cousins have moved to other parts of the country."

Dwaine scratched the side of his head. "Most of my family lives in Montana, and my sister lives in Seattle, Washington. We all keep in touch through phone calls and e-mail."

Sheila nodded and fought the urge to grab a handful of receipts and begin searching for anything that might help find her missing Bye-Lo baby. Her conversation with Dwaine was pleasant, but it wasn't accomplishing a lot.

A few minutes later, Dwaine laid the last piece of paper on top of the stack. "There's nothing here that would indicate a Bye-Lo doll was bought or sold last fall, and these receipts go clear back to the beginning of April that year."

Sheila resented his implication, and she bristled. "Are you suggesting my grandmother just *thought* she brought the doll here and sold it to Bill Summers?"

Dwaine's ears turned pink as he shoved the receipts back into the shoe box. "I'm not saying that at all. Since Bill was so forgetful, it's possible he either didn't write up a receipt or filed it someplace other than the shoe box."

Which is a dumb place to file anything. Sheila forced a smile. "Now what do we do?"

Dwaine patted his stomach. "I don't know about you, but I'm starving. How about we go to the café next door and get some grub? Then, if you have the time, we can come back here and check a few other places."

Sheila's stomach rumbled at the mention of food. She hadn't taken time for lunch this afternoon, and breakfast had consisted of only a cup of coffee and a bagel with cream cheese. A real meal might be just what she needed right now.

She slung her purse over her shoulder. "Dinner sounds good to me."

Dwaine lifted one eyebrow and tipped his head. "Around here it's called supper."

She grinned up at him. "Oh, right. How

28

could I have forgotten something as important as that?"

CHAPTER 3

Casper's Café wasn't the least bit crowded, but this was Wednesday, and Sheila remembered that most people didn't go out to eat in the middle of the week. At least not around these parts.

Sheila studied the menu place mat in front of her, although she didn't know why. She and Dwaine had already placed their orders for sirloin steaks and baked potatoes. It was more than she normally ate, but for some reason Sheila felt ravenous. Maybe it was the company. She felt comfortable sitting here in a cozy booth, inside a quaint restaurant, with a man who had the most gorgeous brown eyes she'd ever seen.

Dwaine smiled from across the table. "You remind me of someone."

"Who?"

He fingered the dimple in his chin. "I'm not sure. Shirley Temple, maybe."

Sheila squinted her eyes. "Shirley Temple

had blond hair, and mine's black as midnight."

"True, but her hair was a mass of curls, and so is yours."

She reached up to touch the uncontrollable tendrils framing her face. Her hair had always been naturally curly, and when she was a child, she'd liked not having to do much with it. Now Sheila simply endured the nasty curls, envying others with straight, sleek hair.

He traced his fingers along the edge of the table. "Do you know what an original Shirley Temple doll is worth on today's market?"

She shook her head.

"Several hundred dollars."

"Wow. That's impressive."

"Your lost Bye-Lo baby's going for a tidy sum, too."

"Really?"

He nodded. "I saw an eighteen-inch Bye-Lo listed in a doll collectors' magazine several weeks ago, and it cost a thousand dollars."

Sheila's mouth fell open. "That's a lot of money. I had no idea the doll was so valuable."

"Actually, the eight-inch version, like your grandmother had, is only selling for five hundred dollars."

"Only?"

"You see that as a bad thing?"

"It is for me, since I don't have the doll or that kind of money lying around."

"We're going to find it," Dwaine said with the voice of assurance, "and it might not cost as much as you think. If the doll's still at my shop, I can sell her back to you for whatever Bill Summers paid your grandmother, which I'm sure wasn't nearly as much as the doll is worth."

Sheila's heart hammered. Why should she be forced to buy something she was told she could have? Of course, Grandma hadn't actually said Sheila could have the doll. It had been sold several months ago, and Grandma probably figured there were lots of other things in the attic Sheila could pick from.

She squeezed her eyes shut, hoping to ward off the threatening tears. It might be childish, but she wanted that doll and nothing else.

"You okay?"

Sheila felt Dwaine's hand cover hers, and her eyes snapped open. "I–I'm fine. If you can find the doll, I'll pay you whatever you think it's worth."

"I'll do my best."

Sheila studied Dwaine's features — the prominent nose, velvet brown eyes, sandy-blond hair, and heavy dark eyebrows. He looked so sincere when he smiled. Hopefully he meant what he said about helping find the precious Bye-Lo baby. Maybe he wasn't like Kevin, who'd offered her nothing but lies and broken promises.

"You mentioned earlier that your folks are missionaries in Brazil."

"Yes. They've been living there for the past year."

"That sounds exciting. My church sent a work and witness team to Argentina last summer. The group said it was a worthwhile experience."

"Are you active in your church?" Sheila questioned.

He reached for his glass of water and grinned at her. "I teach a teen Sunday school class. Ever since I accepted the Lord as my Savior, I've wanted to work with young people." He chuckled. "I was only fourteen at the time of my conversion, so I had to grow up and become an adult before they'd let me teach."

Sheila relaxed against her seat. *Why couldn't I meet someone as nice as you in Fresno?* She shook her head, hoping to get herself thinking straight again. Her vacation would be over in a week, and then she'd be going back to California. It might be some time before she returned to Casper for another visit. Dwaine Woods could be married by then.

"So if your folks live in Brazil and your brother lives in San Diego, what's keeping you in Fresno?" Dwaine asked.

"My job, I guess." Sheila fingered her napkin. What was taking their order so long?

"That's all? Just a job?"

She nodded. "As I said earlier, I work as a receptionist at a chiropractor's office."

Dwaine leaned his elbows on the table and looked at her intently. "You're so pretty, I figure there must be a man in your life."

Sheila felt her face heat up. Was Dwaine flirting with her? He couldn't be; they barely knew each other. "There is no man in my life." *Not anymore.*

She was relieved when their waitress showed up. The last thing she wanted to talk about was her broken engagement to Kevin. She was trying to put the past to rest.

"Sorry it took so long," the middle-aged woman said as she set plates in front of them. "We're short-handed in the kitchen tonight, and I'm doing double duty." There were dark circles under her eyes, and several strands of gray hair crept out of the bun she wore at the back of her neck.

"We didn't mind the wait," Dwaine said. He smiled at Sheila and winked. "It gave me a chance to get better acquainted with this beautiful young woman."

His comment made her cheeks feel warm, and she reached for her glass of water, hoping it might cool her down.

"Would you mind if I prayed before we eat?" he asked when the waitress walked away.

"Not at all." Sheila bowed her head as Dwaine's deep voice sought the Lord's blessing on their meal and beseeched God for His help in finding her grandmother's doll.

Maybe everything would work out all right after all.

Dwaine became more frustrated by the minute. They'd been back at his shop for more than an hour and had looked through every drawer and cubbyhole he could think of. There was no sign of any Bye-Lo doll or even a receipt to show there ever had been one.

"Maybe your grandmother took the doll to another antique shop," he said to Sheila, who was searching through a manila envelope Dwaine had found in the bottom of his desk.

"She said she brought it here."

"Maybe she forgot."

Sheila sighed. "I suppose she could have. Grandma recently turned seventy-five, and her memory might be starting to fade."

Dwaine looked at the antique clock on the wall across the room and grimaced. "It's after nine. Maybe we should call it a night."

She nodded and slipped the envelope back in the drawer. "You're right. It is getting late, and I've taken up enough of your time."

"I don't mind," Dwaine was quick to say. "This whole missing doll thing has piqued my interest. I'm in it till the end."

"If there is an end." Sheila scooted her chair away from the desk and stood. "Since you have no record of the doll ever being here, and we don't know for sure if Grandma even brought it into this shop, I fear my Bye-Lo baby might never be found."

The look of defeat on Sheila's face tore at Dwaine's heartstrings. She'd come all the way from California and used vacation time, and he hated to see her go home empty-handed. He took hold of her hand. "I'm not ready to give up yet. I can check with the other antique shops in town and see if they know anything about the doll."

Her blue eyes brightened, although he noticed a few tears on her lashes. "You'd take that much time away from your business to look for my doll?"

"Searching for treasures is my job."

"Oh, that's right."

He squeezed her fingers. "Why don't you go back to your grandmother's and get a good night's sleep? In the morning, you can come back here and we'll search some more."

She drew in a deep breath. "I'd like that, but I'm not staying with Grandma. I'm staying at a hotel."

"How come?"

"Her apartment at the retirement center is too small. She only has one bedroom."

"But you have other relatives in town, right?"

She nodded. "Jessica and Aunt Marlene. Jessica's painting her kitchen right now, and I'm allergic to paint. And Aunt Marlene is out of town on a cruise."

"Guess a hotel is the best bet for you, then, huh?"

"Yes, and since I'll only be here a short time and got a good deal on the room, I'm fine with it."

He grinned at her. "Great. I'll look forward to seeing you tomorrow, then, Sheila."

"Yes. Tomorrow."

CHAPTER 4

Sheila stood at her second-floor hotel window, staring at the parking lot. She'd slept better last night than she thought she would, going to bed with confidence that her doll would be found. Dwaine had assured her he would locate the missing doll, and for some reason, she believed him. The new owner of The Older the Better seemed honest and genuinely interested in helping her.

Sheila crammed her hands into the pockets of her fuzzy pink robe. *Of course, he could just be in it for the money. Dwaine did tell me the Bye-Lo baby is worth several hundred dollars.*

The telephone rang, and she jumped. Who would be calling her at nine o'clock in the morning? She grabbed the receiver on the next ring. "Hello."

"Sheila, honey, it's Grandma."

"Oh, hi."

"I didn't wake you, did I?"

"No, I was up. Sorry I didn't get by your place last night to drop off the house key. I'll come by later today, okay?"

"No hurry, dear. You'll be here a week and might want to visit the old place again."

Sheila's gaze went to the Bible Dwaine had found. She'd set it on the nightstand by her bed. "Grandma, Dwaine found a Bible on top of the piano yesterday. Would you like me to bring that by when I drop off the key?"

"An *old* Bible?"

"Yes, it's black and kind of tattered."

"That belonged to your grandpa. Guess it didn't get packed. Would you like to have it, Sheila?"

"Don't you want to keep it?"

"Since you haven't been able to locate the Bye-Lo doll, I'd like you to have the Bible."

"I'd be honored to have Grandpa's Bible, but I'm still going to keep looking for the doll."

"That's fine, dear. Speaking of the doll . . . What did you and that nice young man find out yesterday?" Grandma asked. "Did you find a receipt?"

Sheila blanched. How did Grandma know she and Dwaine had spent time together searching for anything that might give some clue as to what had happened to her Bye-Lo baby?

"Sheila, are you still there?"

"Yes, I'm here." Sheila licked her lips. "How did you know I was looking for the doll with the owner of The Older the Better?"

"He called me yesterday afternoon. Said the two of you were going through some papers in his shop."

"It must have been while he was in the back room," Sheila said. "I never heard him call you."

Grandma sneezed and coughed a few times, and Sheila felt immediate concern. "Are you okay? You aren't coming down with a cold, I hope."

She could hear Grandma blowing her nose. "I'm fine. Just my allergies acting up. I think I'm allergic to the new carpet in my apartment here."

Sheila's heart twisted. Grandma shouldn't have been forced to leave the home she loved and move to some cold apartment in a retirement center where the carpet made her sneeze.

"Why don't you come back to Fresno with me for a while?" Sheila suggested. "I live all alone in Mom and Dad's big old house, and if you like it there, you can stay permanently."

"Oh no! I could never move from Casper." There was a pause. "It's kind of you to offer though."

Sheila understood why Grandma had declined. Her roots went deep, as she'd been born and raised in Casper, Wyoming. She had married and brought her children up here as well. Besides, Grandma probably wouldn't be able to adjust to the heat in California, especially during the summer months.

"I understand," Sheila said, "but please feel free to come visit anytime you like."

"Yes, I will." Another pause. "Now back to that young man who's helping you look for my old doll . . ."

"What did Dwaine want when he called you?" Sheila asked.

"Dwaine?"

"The new owner of The Older the Better."

"Oh. I think he did tell me his name, but I must have forgotten it."

Sheila dropped to the bed. So Grandma *was* getting forgetful. Maybe she had taken the doll to some other place. Or maybe Bye-Lo was still in her grandmother's possession.

"How come Dwaine phoned you?" Sheila asked again.

Grandma cleared her throat. "He said you and he were going to eat supper together."

"He called to tell you that?"

"Where did you go, dear?"

"To Casper's Café. It's near his shop."

"How nice. I was hoping you would get out and have a little fun while you're here."

Sheila stifled a yawn. "Grandma, I didn't come back to Casper to have fun. I came to choose something from your attic, remember?"

"Yes, of course, but you're twenty-six years old and don't even have a serious boyfriend." Grandma clucked her tongue. "Why, when I was your age, I was already married and had three children."

"Grandma, I'm fine. I enjoy being single." *Liar. I almost married Kevin and was looking forward to raising a family someday.*

Sheila gripped the phone cord in her right hand. "I don't want to spend the rest of my life alone, but the Lord hasn't brought the right man into my life." *And maybe He never will.*

"You might be too fussy," Grandma said. "Did you ever think about that?"

Sheila swallowed hard. Maybe she was. She'd had many dates over the years, but

43

except for Kevin, she'd had no serious relationships.

She shook her head, trying to clear away the troubling thoughts. "Grandma, why did Dwaine really phone? I'm sure it wasn't to inform you that he and I planned to grab a bite of dinner at Casper's Café."

"Supper, dear. We call it supper around here."

Sheila blew out her breath. "Supper then."

"Let's see . . . I believe he called to ask me some questions about the doll."

Sheila's hopes soared. "Did you remember something that might be helpful?" She didn't recall Dwaine saying anything about his call to Grandma. Surely if he'd discovered some helpful information, he would have told her.

Grandma released a sigh. "I'm afraid not, but he did say he was looking for a receipt."

Sheila jumped off the bed and strode back to the window as an idea popped into her head. "What about your copy of the receipt, Grandma? Didn't Bill Summers give you one when you took the doll in?"

"Hmm . . ." Sheila could almost see her grandmother's expression — dark eyebrows drawn together, forehead wrinkled under her gray bangs, and pink lips pursed in contemplation.

"I suppose I did get a receipt," Grandma admitted, "but I have no idea where I put it. With the mess of moving and all, it could be almost anywhere."

"I see." Sheila couldn't hide her disappointment.

"I've got a suggestion."

"What's that, Grandma?"

"Why don't you go over to The Older the Better again today? You're good at organizing and might be able to help find it."

"I doubt that." Sheila had already spent several hours in Dwaine's shop. The place was a disaster, with nothing organized or filed in the way she would have done had she been running the place.

"Besides," Grandma added, "it will give you a chance to get to know Dwaine better. He's single, you know. Told me so on the phone yesterday."

Sheila's gaze went to the ceiling. Grandma was such a romantic. She remembered how her grandmother used to talk about fixing candlelight dinners for her and Grandpa. Grandma delighted in telling her granddaughters how she believed love and romance were what kept a marriage alive. "That and having the good Lord in the center of your lives," she had said more than once.

Sheila reflected on a special day when Grandma had taken her, Kimber, Lauren, and Jessica shopping. The girls had just been starting into their teen years, and Grandma had bought them each a bottle of perfume, some nail polish, and a tube of lipstick. Then she'd told them how important it was to always look their best in public.

"You never know when you might meet Mr. Right," Grandma had said with a wink. As they drove home that day, Grandma had sung "Some Enchanted Evening."

"Sheila, are you still there?"

Grandma's question drove Sheila's musings to the back of her mind. "Yes, and I will go back to the antique shop today," she replied. "But please don't get any ideas about Dwaine Woods becoming my knight in shining armor."

"Of course not, dear. I'll let you make that decision."

Dwaine whistled as he polished a brass vase that had been brought in last week. It was an heirloom and would sell for a tidy sum if he could find the right buyer. He hoped it would be soon, because business had been slow the last few weeks, and he needed to make enough money to pay the bills that

46

were due.

If I could find that Bye-Lo doll for Sheila, I might have the money I need.

A verse — 1 Timothy 6:10 — popped into Dwaine's head. *"For the love of money is a root of all kinds of evil."*

"I don't really love money, Lord. I just need enough to pay the bills."

Then *"My God will meet all your needs according to the riches of his glory in Christ Jesus,"* from Philippians 4:19, came to mind.

Dwaine placed the vase on a shelf by the front door. He'd done the best he could with it and knew it would sell in God's time. And if he found Sheila's doll, it would be because he was trying to help, not trying to make a profit at her expense.

An image of the dark-haired beauty flashed into his head. Sheila fascinated him, and if she lived in Casper, he would probably make a move toward a relationship with her.

But she lives in California, he reminded himself. *She'll be leaving soon, so I shouldn't allow myself to get emotionally involved with a woman I may never see again.*

The silver bell above the front entrance jingled as the door swung open. Sheila stepped into the store, looking even more beautiful than she had the day before.

Dwaine's palms grew sweaty, and he swallowed hard. So much for his resolve.

"Hi, Sheila. It's good to see you again."

CHAPTER 5

Sheila halted when she stepped through the door. Dwaine stood beside a shelf a few feet away, holding a piece of cloth and looking at her in a most peculiar way.

"Good morning," she said, trying to ignore his piercing gaze. *Is my lipstick smudged? Could I have something caught between my teeth?*

"You look well rested." He smiled, and she felt herself begin to relax.

"The bed wasn't as comfortable as my own, but at least I slept."

"That's usually the way it is. Hotel beds never measure up to one's own mattress."

Dwaine's dark eyes held her captive, and Sheila had to look away.

"Have you had breakfast yet?" he asked. "I've got some cinnamon rolls and coffee in the back room."

"Thanks, but the hotel served a continental breakfast." She took a step forward. "I dropped by to see if you've had any luck locating the Bye-Lo doll or at least a receipt."

"Sorry, but I haven't had time to look this morning." He nodded toward a brass vase on the shelf. "I started my day by getting out some items I acquired a few weeks ago."

Sheila struggled to keep her disappointment from showing. "I suppose I could go visit Grandma or my cousin Jessica, then check back with you later on." She turned toward the door, but Dwaine touched her shoulder.

"Why don't you stick around awhile? I'll give you more boxes to go through, and while you're doing that, I can finish up with what I'm doing here."

She turned around. "You wouldn't mind me snooping through your things?"

Dwaine leaned his head back and released a chuckle that vibrated against the knotty pine walls.

"What's so funny?"

"When you said 'snooping through my things,' I had this vision of you dressed as Sherlock Holmes, scrutinizing every nook and cranny while looking for clues that might incriminate me."

Sheila snickered. "Right. That's me — Miss Private Eye of the West."

"I know we covered quite an area yesterday," Dwaine said, "but there are a lot of boxes in the back room, not to mention two old steamer trunks. If you'd like to start there, I'll keep working in this room, trying to set out a few more things to sell."

"Sounds like a plan." Sheila shrugged out of her jacket and hung it on the coat tree near the front door.

Dwaine nodded toward the back room. "Don't forget about the coffee and cinnamon rolls, in case you change your mind and decide you're hungry."

"Thanks." Sheila headed to the other room as the bell rang, indicating a customer had come in. She glanced over her shoulder and saw an elderly man holding a cardboard box in his hands.

"Here, let me help you with that." Dwaine took the box from the gray-haired man who'd entered his shop and placed it on the counter.

The man's bushy gray eyebrows drew together. "My wife died six months ago, and I've been going through her things." His blue eyes watered, and he sniffed as though trying to hold back tears.

"I'm sorry about your wife, Mr. —"

"Edwards. Sam Edwards." He thrust out

51

his wrinkled hand, and Dwaine reached across the counter to shake it.

"My wife had a thing for old dolls," Sam went on to say. "I have no use for them, and I could use some extra money. If you think they're worth anything and want to buy 'em, that is."

Dwaine rummaged through the box, noting there were three dolls with composition heads and bodies, two wooden-ball-jointed bodies with bisque heads, and an old rubber doll that looked like it was ready for burial. He was sure there was some value in the old dolls — all except the one made of rubber. He could probably make a nice profit if he had the dolls fixed, then sold them at the next doll show held in the area. Still, the dolls might be heirlooms, and he would hate to sell anything that should remain in someone's family.

"Don't you have children or grandchildren who might want your wife's dolls?" Dwaine asked.

Sam shook his head. "Wilma and I never had any kids, and none of my nieces seemed interested when I asked them."

"How much are you needing for the dolls?" Dwaine asked, knowing there would be some cost for the repairs, and he might not get his money back if he paid too much for them.

"A hundred dollars would be fine — if you think that's not too high."

Dwaine shook his head. "Actually, I was thinking maybe two hundred."

Sam's eyebrows lifted. "You mean it?"

"Two hundred sounds fair to me."

"All right then."

Dwaine paid the man, escorted him to the front door, and went back to inspect the dolls now in his possession.

"How's it going?" Sheila asked as she entered the room an hour later. "Are you getting lots done?"

He shrugged. "Not really. A man brought in this box of dolls that belonged to his late wife. I've been trying to decide how much each is worth, which ones will need fixing before I can resell them, and which ones to pitch."

"You wouldn't throw out an old doll!" Sheila looked at him as though he'd pronounced a death sentence on someone.

She hurried over to the counter before Dwaine had a chance to respond. "May I see them?" she asked.

He stepped aside. "Be my guest."

Sheila picked up the rubber doll first. It had seen better days, although she thought there might be some hope for it. The head was hard plastic and marred with dirt, but it wasn't broken. The rubber body was cracked in several places, and a couple of fingers and toes were missing. Sheila didn't know much about doll repairs, but it was obvious the rubber body could not be repaired.

"The ball-jointed dolls need restringing, and all the composition ones could use a new paint job," Dwaine said. "I don't see any hope for the rubber one though."

"But the head's in good shape. Couldn't a new body be made to replace the rotting rubber?" Sheila loved dolls and hated the thought of this one ending up in the garbage.

"Replace it with another rubber body, you mean?"

She shook her head. "I was thinking maybe a cloth one. Even if you could find another rubber body, it would probably be in the same shape as this one."

"My sister lives in Seattle, and there's a doll hospital there. I could take these when I visit Eileen next month for Easter." Dwaine smiled. "Our family always gets together at Easter time to celebrate Christ's resurrection and share a meal together."

Sheila thought about all the Easter dinners she and her family had spent at Grandma and Grandpa Dunmore's over the years. She missed those times, and now that Mom and Dad were on the mission field, unless she went to San Diego to be with her brother, she'd be spending Easter alone.

Dwaine closed the lid on the cardboard box. "I'll worry about these later. Right now, let's see if we can locate your Bye-Lo baby. Unless you've already found something in the back room, that is."

She released a sigh. "Afraid not. I did manage to tidy up the place a bit though."

"You organized?"

Was he irritated with her, or just surprised?

"A little. I took a marking pen and wrote a list of the contents on each box. Then I placed the boxes along one wall, in alphabetical order. I also went through the old trunks, but there was nothing in those except some ancient-looking clothes, which I hung on hangers I found in one of the boxes." She took a quick breath. "I hung the clothes on the wall pegs, and that might help take some of the wrinkles out."

Dwaine released a low whistle. "You've been one busy lady!"

She wondered if he was pleased with her organizational skills or perturbed with her meddling. "I hope you don't mind."

He shook his head. "What's to mind? Your offer to snoop has helped get me more structured. At least in the back room." He nodded toward the front of his shop. "This part still needs a lot of help."

"I'd be glad to come by anytime during my stay in Casper and help you clean and organize."

Dwaine tipped his head to one side. "You're too good to be true, Sheila Nickels."

"I just like to organize."

"I'm glad someone does." He made a sweeping gesture with his hand. "As you can probably tell, neatness isn't my specialty. Guess I'm more comfortable in chaos."

She shrugged but made no comment.

"I think I'll check one more spot for a receipt," Dwaine said. "Then I say we take a break for some lunch."

Sheila had to admit she was kind of hungry. "That sounds fine."

Dwaine marched across the room, pulled open the bottom drawer of a metal filing cabinet, and rummaged through its contents.

Sheila stood to one side, watching the proceedings and itching to start organizing the files alphabetically.

"Bingo!" Dwaine held up a receipt and

smiled. "This has got to be it, Sheila."

She studied the piece of paper and read the scrawled words out loud. "Bye-Lo doll, in good condition: Sold to Weber's Antiques, 10 South Union Avenue, Casper, Wyoming." Sheila frowned. "There's no date, so we don't know when Bill Summers sold Grandma's doll."

Dwaine scratched the side of his head. "How about we take a ride over to Weber's? It's on the other side of town, and there's a good hamburger place nearby."

"Why not just phone them?"

He shook his head. "It'll be better if we go in person. That way, if Tom Weber doesn't still have the doll, you can show him the picture you have, and he'll know if that's the same doll we're looking for."

Sheila blew out an exasperated breath. "Of course it's the same doll." She pointed to the receipt in his hands. "It says right here that it's a Bye-Lo."

He nodded. "True, but it might not be the same one your grandmother sold to Bill Summers."

She shrugged. "Okay, let's go find out."

CHAPTER 6

Sheila leaned her elbows on the table and scowled at the menu in front of her. They'd paid a visit to Weber's Antique Shop but had come up empty-handed. After looking at the receipt Dwaine showed him and checking his own records, Tom Weber had informed them he'd received a Bye-Lo doll several months ago but had sold it to a doll collector in town. He'd been kind enough to give them the woman's address, and Dwaine had eagerly agreed to drive over to Mrs. Davis's place to see if she had the doll. After going there, Dwaine had suggested they stop for a bite to eat.

"I can see by the scowl on your face that you're fretting about the doll and the fact we still haven't found it."

Dwaine's statement jolted Sheila out of her contemplations. "I was just thinking we're no further ahead than when we first started."

He shook his head. "I don't see it that way. We found a receipt for a Bye-Lo doll, discovered it had been sold to Weber's Antiques, who in turn sold it to Mrs. Davis, who said she'd originally planned to make new clothes for it and then sell it at the next doll show she went to."

"Then she ended up giving it to her niece for her birthday, but the girl's in school right now so we can't even check on that lead." Sheila pursed her lips as she thought about how much Grandma's doll meant to her. However, she wasn't sure she could take the doll away from a child, even though she would be offering payment.

Dwaine reached for his glass of iced tea. "Let's eat lunch and get to know each other better; then we'll drive over to Amy Davis's house at three thirty, which is when her aunt said she should be home from school."

"I suppose we could do that, but it's only one now. What do we do between the time we finish eating and three thirty?"

"How about we return to my shop, where I can wait for potential customers and you can do more organizing?" He wiggled his eyebrows. "My place is such a mess, and you've done a great job so far in helping get things straightened out."

She smiled in spite of her disappointment

over not yet finding Grandma's doll. She had made Dwaine's antique shop look better, and if given the chance, she probably could put the whole place in order.

Dwaine whistled as he washed the front window of his store. It was more enjoyable to clean and organize when he had help. Sheila was at the back of the store, putting some old books in order according to the authors' last names. Dwaine thought it was kind of silly, since this wasn't the public library, but if it made her happy, he was okay with the idea. Besides, it allowed him more time to be with her. He didn't think it was merely Sheila's dark, curly hair and luminous blue eyes that had sparked his interest either. His attraction to Sheila went much deeper than her physical beauty. She was a Christian, which was the most important thing. Dwaine knew dating a nonbeliever was not in God's plan.

When he heard Sheila singing "Jesus Loves Me," Dwaine smiled and hummed along. When the song ended, he shook his head. *She and I are complete opposites. She likes to organize; I'm a slob. She says "dinner"; I say "supper." She's from sunny California; I'm from windy Wyoming. Still, during the time we've spent together, she has made me feel so complete.*

The grandfather clock struck three, and Dwaine set his roll of paper towels and bottle of cleaner aside. "I think we should head over to Amy Davis's place," he called to Sheila. "She should be home from school by the time we get there."

Sheila strolled across the room. "Are you sure you have time for this, Dwaine? If you keep closing your shop, you might lose all your customers."

He shook his head. "Nah, I'll leave a note saying what time I plan to return, and they'll come back if they were here for anything important."

She eyed him curiously. "Don't you worry about money?"

He shrugged. "It does help pay the bills, but I've come to realize money can't be my primary concern."

"Why are you in business for yourself then?"

"I like what I do." He smiled. "And if I can make a fairly decent living, that's all that matters."

"But you won't even do that if you keep closing your shop."

"Not to worry, Sheila. I'm enjoying the time spent with you."

She blushed. "At first I thought you were

only helping me so you could make some money, but since the doll's not in your shop, if we do find her, there's really nothing in it for you."

He grabbed his jacket off the coat tree. "What can I say? I'm just a nice guy trying to help a damsel in distress."

Sheila climbed the steep steps leading to the home of Amy Davis. It was a grand old place and reminded her of Grandma's house. A small balcony protruded from the second floor, and Sheila couldn't help wondering if that might be Amy's room. *Any girl would love to have a balcony off her bedroom. I know I would.*

When Sheila heard a *thunk,* she glanced over her shoulder. To her shock, she discovered Dwaine lying on the bottom step, holding his leg. Her heart lurched, and she rushed to his side. "What happened?"

He groaned. "I was so intent on looking at Mrs. Davis's historical-looking house that I wasn't watching where I was going and missed a step. Fell flat, and I think I sprained my ankle."

Sheila felt immediate concern when she looked at his ankle, already starting to swell. "If you hadn't been traipsing all over town trying to help me find my grandmother's doll, this never would have happened. What if it's broken? What if you can't work because of the fall?"

Dwaine smiled, even though he was obviously in pain. "I'm sure it's not broken, and it's definitely not your fault." He winced as he tried to stand.

"Here, let me help you." Sheila offered her arm, and Dwaine locked his elbow around hers. "I'd better drive you to the hospital so you can have that ankle x-rayed."

He shook his head. "Not yet."

"What do you mean, not yet? In case it is broken, you need immediate care."

"Just help me to the car. I'll wait there while you speak to Amy Davis."

"Are you kidding me? I can't leave you alone while I go running off to see about a doll that might never be mine."

He hopped on one foot and opened the car door on the passenger's side. "We're here, it's three thirty, and you need to know once and for all if your grandmother's doll is still around."

"But Amy might not want to part with it, and I can't fault her for that."

Dwaine slid into the seat and grimaced. "Ouch."

"Are you sure you're going to be okay?"

"I'll be fine. Now please go knock on the

door and find out if the doll's here or not."

Sheila looked up at the stately home, then back at Dwaine again, and sighed. "I'll only be a few minutes, and as soon as I'm done, we're going to the hospital."

He saluted her. "Whatever you say, ma'am."

Sheila closed the car door and made her way up the long flight of stairs. *I'm surprised it wasn't me who fell. I was studying this grand home, too, and it could have been my ankle that was injured instead of Dwaine's.*

A few seconds later, she stood on the front porch and rang the doorbell. While she waited, she glanced down at her rental car. At least Dwaine hadn't wasted his gasoline on this trip.

Finally, the door opened and a middle-aged woman with light brown hair greeted her with a smile. "May I help you?"

"I'm looking for Amy Davis."

"I don't believe I've met you before. Do you know my daughter?"

Sheila extended her hand. "I'm Sheila Nickels, and I'm in Casper visiting my grandmother who lives at Mountain Springs Retirement Center."

The woman shook Sheila's hand, but her wrinkled forehead revealed obvious confusion. "I'm not sure what that has to do with Amy."

Sheila quickly explained about her visit to Grandma's attic, the missing Bye-Lo doll, and how she and Dwaine had gotten Amy's name and address.

"Let me get this straight," Mrs. Davis said. "You believe the doll Amy's aunt gave her might actually be your grandmother's doll?"

"Yes, I think it's quite possible."

Mrs. Davis opened the door wider. "Please, come in."

Sheila took one last look at the car. She could see Dwaine leaning against the headrest, and a wave of guilt washed over her. She should be driving him to the hospital now, not taking time to see about a doll. *But I'm here,* she reminded herself, *and Dwaine insisted he was okay, so I may as well see what I can find out.*

"Have a seat in the living room and I'll get my daughter." Mrs. Davis ascended the stairs just off the hallway, while Sheila meandered into the other room and positioned herself on the couch. It was near the front window, so she could keep an eye on Dwaine. *I hope his leg's not broken, and I pray he isn't in much pain.* Sheila hated to admit it, but the carefree antique dealer was working his way into her heart, even though she'd only met him yesterday. It wasn't like her to have strong feelings for someone she barely knew. She, who had kept her heart well guarded since her broken engagement to Kevin.

Sheila heard the floor creak, and she snapped her attention away from the window, turning toward the noise. A teenaged girl with hazel-colored eyes and long blond hair gazed at her with a curious expression. "I'm Amy Davis. My mother said you wanted to speak to me and that you were interested in the doll my aunt gave me for my birthday."

Sheila nodded. "Yes, that's right."

"I hope you're not planning to take the Bye-Lo away, because I collect dolls, and she's special to me."

"I — I just want to see her. I need to know if she's the same doll my grandma used to have in her attic." Sheila didn't have the heart to tell Amy that if it was Grandma's doll, she planned to offer payment to get it back.

"Hang on a minute." Amy whirled around and hurried out of the room. A short time later she was back, holding a small cardboard box in her hands. She set it on the coffee table in front of the couch and opened the lid. Carefully, almost reverently, she lifted the doll and cradled it in her arms as though it were a real baby.

Sheila's heart hammered. It sure looked like Grandma's doll. It was the same size and had the exact shade of brown painted on its pink porcelain head, and the doll's hands were made of celluloid. "May I have a closer look?"

With a reluctant expression, Amy handed Sheila the doll. "Be careful with her. She's breakable."

"Yes, I know." Sheila placed the Bye-Lo baby in her lap and lifted her white nightgown.

"What are you doing?" Amy's eyes were huge, and she looked horror-struck.

"I want to see if there's any writing on her tummy."

Amy dropped to the couch beside Sheila. "Why would there be writing? I never wrote anything on the doll."

"If this is my grandmother's, then my name should be on the stomach. I wrote it there when I was a little girl, hoping some-day the doll would be mine." Sheila pulled the small flannel diaper aside, but there was no writing. Part of her felt a sense of relief. At least she wouldn't be faced with having to ask Amy to give up a doll she obviously cared about. Another part of her was sad.

Since this wasn't Grandma's doll, then where was she?

Sheila smoothed the clothes back into place and handed the Bye-Lo to Amy. "It's not my grandmother's doll, and I apologize for having troubled you."

Amy's mother stepped into the room just then. "It was no bother." She walked Sheila to the door. "I hope you find your grandmother's doll. I suspect it meant a lot to you."

Sheila could only nod in reply, for she was afraid if she spoke she might break down in tears. It was clear she wasn't going to locate the missing doll, and now she had to take Dwaine to the hospital to have his ankle checked out. All she'd accomplished today was getting Dwaine hurt and making herself feel more depressed. *Maybe I never should have come back to Casper. Maybe I'm not supposed to have that doll.*

CHAPTER 7

For the next week, Sheila divided her time between Mountain Springs Retirement Center, to see Grandma, and The Older the Better Antique Shop, to help Dwaine. After his ankle had been x-rayed, the doctor determined that it wasn't broken but he'd sprained it badly. Dwaine would be hobbling around on crutches for a couple of weeks, which would make it difficult to wait on customers, much less stock shelves, clean, or organize things in his shop. Since Sheila felt responsible for the accident, she'd called her boss and asked if she could take her last two weeks of vacation now. Dr. Taylor agreed, saying the woman he'd hired in Sheila's absence was available to help awhile longer and telling Sheila to enjoy the rest of her time off. Since Sheila couldn't afford another week or two at a hotel, after speaking with Grandma, she decided to stay in her grandmother's old house until she felt ready to leave Casper. There was still enough furniture for her to get by, and since the power was on, she figured she could manage okay.

"This is so much fun," she muttered under her breath as she dumped another load of trash into the wastebasket near Dwaine's desk. Every day this week when she'd been helping Dwaine, Sheila had continued to search for Grandma's doll or a receipt. No amount of cleaning or organizing revealed any evidence that the doll had ever been in Dwaine's store. Dwaine had phoned all the other antique shops in town, but no one had any record of her grandmother's doll. Sheila felt sure it was hopeless.

"I'd like to meet your grandmother in person and ask a few more questions about the doll," Dwaine said as he hobbled up to Sheila on his crutches.

"That's a great idea. Grandma's been wanting to meet you, and I happen to know she baked a batch of peanut butter cookies yesterday afternoon."

He wiggled his eyebrows. "One of my all-time favorites."

Sheila smiled at Dwaine's enthusiasm. He reminded her of a little boy. During the past week, she'd gotten to know him better. His lackadaisical attitude and disorganization bothered her some, but he had a certain charm that captivated her. Not only was Dwaine good looking, but he seemed so kind and compassionate. Several times she'd seen him deal with customers, and always he'd been polite and fair in his business dealings. Even though Sheila knew little about antiques, she could tell by the customers' reactions how pleased they were with the prices he quoted.

"So when do we leave?"

Dwaine's question halted Sheila's musings, and she gazed up at him. "Oh, you mean go to Grandma's place?"

He nodded and grinned at her. "That's where the peanut butter cookies are, right?"

"Yes. I just didn't realize you wanted to go there this minute."

"Business has been slow this morning, so there's no time like the present."

Sheila was tempted to say something about Dwaine's overly casual manner, but she decided it was none of her business how he handled things at his shop.

He made his way across the room and reached for his jacket. In the process, the coat tree nearly fell over, and Sheila was afraid Dwaine might lose his balance, too. With one hand she grabbed the wobbly object; with the other she took hold of Dwaine's arm. "Better let me help you with your jacket."

As soon as they had their coats on, she opened the front door, stepped outside, and headed for her rental.

"I've always wondered how it would feel to have a chauffeur," Dwaine said in a teasing voice. "Since I sprained my ankle, it's been kind of nice having you drive me around."

Dwaine had never been to Mountain Springs Retirement Center, but when they pulled into the parking lot, he was impressed with the facilities. The grounds were well cared for and included numerous picnic tables, wooden benches, bird feeders, and a couple of birdbaths.

When they entered the building, he noticed the foyer was decorated with several green plants, and a huge fish tank was built into one wall.

Sheila led the way, walking slowly down a long corridor and up the elevator to the third floor. Soon they were standing in front of a door with Lydia Dunmore's name engraved on a plaque.

A few minutes after Sheila knocked, the door opened. A slightly plump elderly woman with her hair styled in a short bob greeted them with a smile. Her blue eyes sparkled, the same way Sheila's did, and she held out her arms. "Sheila, what a nice surprise!"

Sheila giggled and embraced the woman. "Grandma, you know I've dropped by here nearly every day since I came back to Casper. I don't see how my being here now can be such a surprise."

"Of course not, dear, but this is the first time you've shown up with a man at your side." She glanced over at Dwaine and smiled. "And such a nice-looking one, too."

Dwaine's ears burned from her scrutiny, and he noticed Sheila's face had turned crimson as well.

"Grandma, this is Dwaine Woods, the new owner of The Older the Better Antique Shop."

"It's nice to meet you in person. I'm Lydia Dunmore." She held out her hand.

Dwaine was surprised at the strength of Lydia's handshake. "It's good to meet you, Mrs. Dunmore."

"Lydia. Please call me Lydia."

He nodded in reply.

"Sheila told me about your ankle. How are you doing?"

"Getting along quite well, thanks to your

granddaughter helping out at my shop."

"Glad to hear that. So now, to what do I owe the privilege of this visit?" she asked, motioning them inside her apartment.

"I heard you made some cookies," Dwaine blurted.

Sheila nudged him gently in the ribs. "I can't believe you said that."

"Me neither." Dwaine shook his head. "The words slipped out before I had time to think. Sorry about that, Mrs. — I mean, Lydia."

She chuckled and headed for the small kitchen area. "You remind me of my late husband. He always said exactly what was on his mind."

Sheila pulled out a wooden stool at the snack bar for Dwaine and took his crutches, placing them nearby. "Have a seat. Grandma loves to entertain, so I'm sure she can't wait to serve us."

Sheila studied Dwaine's profile as he leaned his elbows on the counter and made easy conversation with Grandma.

"Yes, ma'am," he said in answer to Grandma's most recent question. "I've gone to church ever since I was a boy. Accepted the Lord as my Savior when I was a teenager, and now I teach a teen Sunday school class."

Grandma piled a plate high with peanut butter cookies and placed it in front of Dwaine. Then she poured a tall glass of milk and handed it to him.

"Hey, don't I get any?" Sheila stuck out her lower lip in an exasperated pout.

"Don't worry your pretty little head." Grandma put half as many cookies on another plate, poured a second glass of milk, and handed them to Sheila.

Before Sheila could voice the question, Grandma said, "What can I say? He's a growing boy with a sprained ankle and needs more cookies than you do."

Dwaine patted his stomach. "If I'm not careful, I'll be growing fat."

"You could use a little more meat on your bones." Grandma glanced at Sheila. "Don't you think so, dear?"

Sheila's face flamed. She thought Dwaine looked fine the way he was. A bit too fine, maybe. She sure wasn't going to admit that to her grandmother though.

Searching for a change of subject, Sheila said, "Dwaine and I have looked high and low for anything that would show you took the Bye-Lo doll to his shop, but we haven't found a thing."

Grandma tipped her head to one side. "Guess you'd better make another trip to my attic."

"I appreciate the offer, but as I told you before, there's nothing else I want." Sheila took a bite of her cookie. "Mmm . . . this is good."

"Thanks." Grandma grinned and snatched a cookie from Sheila's plate. "I'm glad you two stopped by so I didn't have to eat them all myself."

"I was wondering if you've had the chance to look at my appraisal of your piano," Dwaine said.

Grandma's forehead wrinkled. "Your offer sounds fair, Dwaine, but to tell you the truth, I'm having a hard time parting with that old relic. I've had it since I was a girl."

Dwaine swallowed the last of his milk. "Too bad there isn't room for it here."

Tears welled up in Grandma's eyes. "Even if I could have had it moved to this apartment, I don't think the others who live here would appreciate my playing it. These walls aren't soundproof, you know."

"There's a piano downstairs in the game room," Sheila said. "Grandma can play that whenever she wants."

"Maybe someone in your family would like to buy the piano," Dwaine said.

Grandma smiled. "I'll have to ask around."

Dwaine looked at Sheila. "One good thing

has come from hunting for the missing doll."

"Oh, what's that?"

"I've gotten to know you."

"The man has a point," Grandma put in. "I can tell by the way you two look at each other that you're a match made in heaven."

"Grandma, please!" Sheila knew her face must be bright red, because she felt heat travel up the back of her neck and cascade onto her cheeks.

"You look a little flushed, dear. I hope you're not coming down with something."

"I think Sheila's embarrassed by your last statement," Dwaine said, coming to Sheila's rescue.

Grandma looked sheepish. "Sorry about that."

"Dwaine and I barely know each other," Sheila said. "I think you're a romantic at heart, Grandma."

Grandma grinned. "Your grandpa and I got married after knowing each other only one month, and we had a wonderful marriage. It's always been my desire that each of my children and grandchildren find a suitable mate and know the kind of happiness Grandpa and I had." She winked at Dwaine. "Sheila's more priceless than any of my attic treasures, so don't let her get away."

CHAPTER 8

Sheila and Dwaine drove back to his shop in silence. He was busy writing something in a notebook he'd taken from his jacket pocket, and she needed time to think. Was Grandma right about her and Dwaine? Were they a match made in heaven? Could it be that God had brought Sheila back to Casper to begin a relationship with Dwaine, not for the Bye-Lo baby?

Sheila gripped the steering wheel as a ball of anxiety rolled in the pit of her stomach. *No, it couldn't be. If I allow myself to fall for this man, one of us would have to move. A long-distance relationship won't work. Kevin proved that when he moved to Oregon and sent me a letter saying he'd met someone else.*

As though he sensed she was thinking about him, Dwaine looked over at her and smiled. "It's almost noon, and I'm getting kind of hungry. Should we stop for lunch somewhere?"

Sheila focused on the road ahead. "After all those cookies you ate at Grandma's, I wouldn't think you'd have any room for lunch."

"Aw, those only whetted my appetite."

She snickered. "Yeah, I could tell."

"Seriously, I would like to take you to lunch."

"How about I pay for the meal today? You bought me dinner — I mean, supper — a couple times last week and only let me leave the tip." She clucked her tongue. "And that was just because I threatened to make a scene if you didn't."

Dwaine tapped the notebook against his knee. "You really don't have to even things out. I enjoy your company, and while our meals aren't exactly dates, I find myself wishing they were."

Sheila's heart pounded, and her hands became sweaty. "You do?"

"Yep. In fact, I've been working up the nerve to ask if you'd go out with me."

"You mean something more than supper?"

"Right. A real date, where I come to your grandma's old place and pick you up."

"Where would we go?" Sheila hadn't meant to enjoy his company so much. She'd be leaving Casper soon, and then what?

79

"I thought maybe we could take in a show. A couple of good movies are playing right now, and tonight there shouldn't be a lot of people."

"But this is Monday — a weeknight," she reminded.

"And?"

"You'll need to get up early tomorrow for work." Sheila was an early to bed, early to rise kind of person, and it was a good thing. Dr. Taylor opened his chiropractic clinic at eight o'clock, five mornings a week, and Sheila had never been late to work.

"I own my own business, which means I can set my own hours," Dwaine replied.

"Still, maybe we should wait until Friday to go out."

"I don't want to wait that long. You'll be leaving for California soon, and we shouldn't waste the time you have left."

Sheila's heart skipped a beat. "You've seen me nearly every day for the last two weeks."

"Those weren't dates. That was business." He touched her arm, and even through her jacket she felt warm tingles.

Sheila stared at the road ahead. She had to keep her focus on driving, not Dwaine. The truth was, except for his disorganization, he had all the attributes she was looking for in a man. Dwaine appeared to be kind, gentle, caring, humorous — and as a bonus, he was good-looking — but most important, he was a Christian.

"You haven't said if you'll go out with me tonight or not," he prompted.

Sheila took a deep breath and threw caution to the wind. "Sure, why not? Since we can't seem to find Grandma's doll, I may as well make good use of my time spent here."

A knock at the door let Sheila know her date had arrived. She took one last look in the hall mirror and hurried to answer it, hoping she looked okay. She'd decided to wear a long black skirt and a pale blue blouse, which she knew brought out the color of her eyes.

When she opened the door, Sheila's breath caught in her throat. Dwaine was dressed in a pair of beige slacks and a black leather jacket, and a bouquet of pink and white carnations was tucked under one arm. "The flowers are for you, pretty lady."

Since Dwaine's hands gripped his crutches, Sheila reached for the bouquet. "Thanks. They're beautiful." She scanned the room, looking for something to put the flowers in. "I'd better get a glass of water from the kitchen. I'm pretty sure Grandma's vases have all been packed away, because I haven't seen any in the kitchen cupboards."

When Sheila returned a few seconds later, she set the glass of water on the small table in the entryway and placed the flowers inside.

"You look beautiful tonight," Dwaine said, offering her a wide smile.

"You don't look so bad yourself."

"Ready to go?"

She nodded and grabbed her coat from the closet, but before she could put it on, Dwaine set his crutches aside and took it from her. "Here, let me help you with that."

"You're going to fall over if you're not careful."

"Nah. I'm gettin' good at doing things on one foot."

As Sheila slipped her arms inside the sleeves, she shivered.

"You cold?"

"No, not really." She buttoned the coat and opened the door. "What time does the show start?"

"Not until seven thirty. I thought we'd start with dinner at a nice restaurant, then follow it with the movies."

Sheila snickered. "You just said 'dinner' instead of 'supper.' "

He winked. "This is a date. Gentlemen take their ladies out to dinner, not supper."

■ ■ ■ ■

Sheila hated to see her date with Dwaine end. Dinner had been delicious, the show had been great, and she'd enjoyed every minute spent in his company. Now they stood on Grandma's front porch, about to say good night.

"I had a good time tonight. Thanks," Sheila said.

"Yeah, me, too." His voice was husky, and his dark eyes held her captive. "How about a drive to the country tomorrow during our lunch break? I can get chicken to go from Casper's Café."

She licked her lips. "That sounds good. I love fried chicken."

There was an awkward pause; then Dwaine lowered his head and his lips sought hers. The kiss was gentle and soft, lasting only a few seconds, but it took Sheila's breath away. Things were happening too fast, and her world was tilting precariously.

"Good night. See you tomorrow," Dwaine murmured before she had a chance to say anything. He hobbled down the steps, leaving Sheila with a racing heart and a head full of tangled emotions as she shut the door.

She'd been caught up in the enjoyment of the evening and had let him kiss her. "I've got to call a halt to this before one of us gets hurt," she mumbled at her reflection in the mirror. "Even though I enjoy Dwaine's company and believe he's a true Christian, a long-distance relationship will never work. I'll tell him in the morning that I'd rather not take a drive to the country."

Somewhere in the distance an annoying bell kept ringing. Pulling herself from the haze of sleep, Sheila slapped her hand on the clock by the antique bed in Grandma's guest room. "It can't be time to get up. It seems like I just went to bed."

The ringing continued, and she finally realized it was the phone and not her alarm. She grabbed for the receiver. "Hello."

"Hi, Sheila, it's Dwaine. When you didn't show up at nine this morning, I started to worry. Are you okay?"

Sheila stifled a yawn and rolled out of bed. "I'm fine." She glanced at the clock and cringed when she realized it was almost ten o'clock. "Sorry, guess I overslept and must have forgotten to set the alarm."

"That's okay, but I've got some news to share when you get here."

"Can't you tell me now? I'm curious."

Sheila stretched and reached for her fuzzy pink robe.

"I stayed up last night reading some doll collectors' magazine I recently bought, and I think I may have found your missing doll."

She flopped onto the bed, draping the robe across her legs. "Really? What makes you think it's the one?"

"It fits the description you gave me, and there's some writing on the doll's cloth body. Could be your name, Sheila."

She sucked in her breath. *Maybe the trip to Casper hasn't been a waste of time after all.* Her conscience pricked her. *How could I even think such a thing? Grandma's here, and I've enjoyed spending time with her — Dwaine, too, for that matter.*

"Sheila, are you still there?"

"Yes, yes. You really think you've found my grandma's doll?"

"There's no way to be sure until you take a look at the magazine." There was a brief pause, and Sheila thought she heard the bell above the door of Dwaine's store jingle. "A customer just walked in, so I'd better go," he said. "If you can come over as soon as possible, we'll have time to check out the doll information before we go for our drive."

Sheila clutched the folds in her robe. "About our picnic date —"

"Gotta go. See you soon, Sheila."

There was a click, and the telephone went dead. Sheila blew out her breath and placed the phone back on the table. Even though she was a bit put out with Dwaine for hanging up so abruptly, she felt a sense of elation over the possibility that he might have actually found Grandma's doll.

For the next hour, when Dwaine wasn't waiting on customers, he watched the door, anxious for Sheila to arrive. He was excited to show her the information about the Bye-Lo doll in the magazine he'd found, but more than that, he looked forward to seeing Sheila again. After their date last night, he was convinced he wanted to begin a relationship with her.

Dwaine snapped the cash register drawer shut and shook his head. *This is ridiculous. I can't be falling for someone who lives three states away. Would Sheila be willing to relocate? I don't think I could live in California.*

The bell above the door jingled as one customer left the store and another entered. It was Sheila, wearing a pair of blue jeans with a matching jacket. "Have you got time to show me that doll magazine?" she asked.

"Sure. There's a lull between customers, so come on back." Dwaine motioned for

Sheila to follow him over to his desk in one corner of the room. He leaned his crutches against the side of the desk and took a seat. She sat in the straight-backed oak chair nearby.

Dwaine pointed to the magazine. "Here's the Bye-Lo that caught my attention. Don't you think she looks like your grandmother's old doll?"

Sheila jumped out of her chair and leaned over his shoulder. "That does look like her, but I can't be sure. I wish the writing on the doll's stomach was clearer."

Dwaine stared at the picture. "Guess I'd better contact the person who placed this ad and ask what the writing says."

"It might be good to find out how much they're asking for the doll, too." Sheila blew out her breath, and he shivered as it tickled his neck.

"I want that doll really bad, but if it's going to cost too much, I may have to pass."

"After all the searching we've done, you can't walk away if this is your grandmother's doll. I'm sure we can work something out."

"I'm serious, Dwaine. Besides paying for the doll, I'll have to cover the cost of your services."

He swiveled his chair, bumping heads with her in the process.

"Ouch!"

"I'm so sorry." He wrapped his arms around her, and she fell into his lap.

Sheila let out a gasp, but he covered her mouth with his before she could protest. His lips were soft, warm, and inviting. She responded by threading her fingers through the back of his hair.

Dwaine wished the kiss could have gone on forever, but the spell was broken when another customer entered the store.

Sheila jerked her head back and jumped up. Her face was the shade of a ripe Red Delicious apple.

"I–I'd better get to work. I've got a lot more cleaning to do in the back room." She stumbled away from Dwaine.

"We'll stop work at noon so we can take our drive to the country with a picnic lunch," he called after her.

"I've changed my mind and decided not to go."

The door to the storage room clicked shut before Dwaine could say anything more. He turned to the elderly woman who had entered the shop and forced a smile. "May I help you, ma'am?"

CHAPTER 9

Sheila paced back and forth, from the living room window of Grandma's old house to the couch, still covered by a sheet. She'd left The Older the Better almost two hours ago and hadn't heard a word from Dwaine. He'd said he would call her tonight if he heard from the doll collector.

Of course, she reasoned, *it might take days for him to get a reply about the doll. But I'll be leaving soon, and then what?*

The phone rang in the kitchen, and Sheila rushed out of the room to get it. "Dwaine?" she asked breathlessly into the receiver.

"No, it's Grandma."

"Oh, hi." Sheila stared out the back window into the neighbor's yard. A young couple with a baby was getting into their car. Her heart took a nosedive. Would she ever fall in love, get married, and have children?

"Sheila, did you hear what I said?"

She jerked her gaze away from the window. "What was that, Grandma?"

"I asked if you would like to have supper at my place tonight with Dwaine."

"Thanks for the invite, but I'm not in the mood to eat with the group at the retirement center."

"I wasn't planning to eat downstairs," Grandma said.

"You weren't?"

"No. I hoped to try out a recipe I found in a magazine, and I wanted to cook it for someone besides myself."

Sheila laughed. "You're needing a guinea pig, huh?"

"Actually, I'd prefer to have two guinea pigs."

Sheila groaned. "Grandma, you're not trying to play matchmaker, are you?"

Grandma cleared her throat and gave a polite little cough. "Of course not, dear. What would give you that idea?"

Sheila thought about telling Grandma how she and Dwaine had made a date for this afternoon and how she'd changed her mind about going. If she invited Dwaine to join her for supper at Grandma's, it would be like sending him mixed signals.

"Sheila, please don't say no. You'll be leaving next week, and I'd like to spend as much time with you as possible before you go." Grandma's tone was kind of pathetic, and Sheila figured she would feel guilty for days if she turned down the invitation.

Sheila shifted the phone from one ear to the other. "Okay, I'll come, but let's make it just the two of us. I'm sure Dwaine is busy."

"No, he's not. I already invited him."

Sheila flopped into the closest chair at the table. "You asked him first?"

There was a pause. "I was afraid you might refuse."

"Dwaine and I aren't right for each other. So you may as well give up your match-maker plans."

Grandma chuckled. "Who are you trying to convince, sweet girl? Me or yourself?"

"I live in California, and Dwaine lives here in Wyoming. A long-distance relationship would never work."

"One of you could move."

"My job is there, and his is here."

"Have you prayed about this?"

Sheila hated to admit it, but she hadn't. It wasn't like her not to pray about a situation she knew only the Lord could resolve.

Grandma clucked her tongue. "Your silence tells me you probably haven't taken this matter to God. Am I right?"

"Yes, Grandma, you're right."

"I think you're making excuses and should give the situation serious thought, as well as a lot of prayer. Jobs are to be had in every town, you know."

Sheila drew in a deep breath and released it with a moan. "I'll admit, I am attracted to Dwaine, but I don't know why, because we're as different as east is from west."

"How so?"

"For one thing, I'm a neat freak; I'm always organizing."

"I can't argue with that. The last time you dropped by, you organized my kitchen cupboards so well I couldn't find anything for two days."

"According to Dwaine, his shop was a mess when he bought it, but to tell you the truth, I'm not sure he is much better about organization than the previous owner," Sheila said, ignoring her grandmother's teasing comment. "That receipt for your old doll is probably someplace in his shop, and we can't unearth it because of all the clutter."

"I would think with your ability to organize, you'd have found the doll or a receipt if it was still there."

"I've checked everywhere I could think of, and so has Dwaine."

"I'm sorry you came all this way to get

one of my attic treasures, and now you'll be going home empty-handed."

"I guess the doll's not really that important, and I do have Grandpa's Bible." As the words slipped off her tongue, Sheila knew she hadn't really meant them. Would she be okay going home without the Bye-Lo baby? Could she return to California and never think of Dwaine Woods again? Would his kisses be locked away in her heart forever?

"Sure wish you'd consider taking something else from the attic," Grandma said. "I could come over to the old house tomorrow and help check things out."

Sheila shook her head, although she didn't know why; Grandma couldn't see the action. "Actually, Dwaine might have another lead on the doll."

"Really? Why didn't you say so before?"

"He found a Bye-Lo baby advertised in a doll collectors' magazine, and it looks like your old doll. There's even some writing on the cloth body, but it could be another false lead."

"Writing? Why would there be writing on the doll?"

Sheila's face heated with embarrassment. She'd been only eight years old when she wrote her name on the doll's stomach, but

93

she'd never told Grandma what she'd done.

"I — uh — am sorry to say that I wrote my name on Bye-Lo's tummy when I was a little girl."

"Whatever for?"

"Because I wanted her to be mine someday, and I hoped maybe . . ." Sheila's voice trailed off.

"Oh, I see."

"It was a stupid, childish thing to do, and I'm sorry, Grandma."

"Apology accepted." Grandma chuckled. "Who knows, your name might be the very thing that helps you know for sure if it's my doll or not."

"That's why I'm hoping the person who placed the ad responds to Dwaine's phone call soon."

"While you're waiting to hear, won't you join me and Dwaine for supper this evening?"

Sheila nearly choked. "He said yes?"

"Sure did. Now how 'bout you, dear? Will you come, too?"

Sheila felt like she was backed into a corner, but she didn't want to disappoint Grandma. "What time should I be there?"

"Six o'clock. Dwaine will pick you up at a quarter to."

"You arranged that as well?" Sheila's voice

rose a notch.

"What else are grandmas for?" Grandma giggled like a young girl. "See you tonight, and wear something pretty."

Sheila lifted her gaze toward the ceiling. "Sure, Grandma."

At a quarter to six, Dwaine arrived at Lydia Dunmore's stately old house to pick up Sheila. His ankle felt somewhat better, so he'd left his crutches at home. He lifted his hand to knock on the door, but it swung open before his knuckles connected with the wood.

"I saw you through the peephole," Sheila said before he could voice the question.

"Ah, so you were waiting for me." He chuckled, and she blushed.

"I'll grab my sweater and then we can go." Sheila disappeared into the living room and returned with a fuzzy blue sweater. Instead of blue jeans and a sweatshirt, like she'd had on today, she was dressed in a pale blue dress that touched her ankles.

"I felt bad when you didn't want to drive to the country this afternoon," Dwaine said as they headed down the steps side by side.

She halted when they came to the sidewalk and turned to face him. "I didn't think it was a good idea for us to go on another date."

He opened his mouth to comment, but she cut him off.

"For that matter, I don't think tonight is such a good idea, either, but I'm doing it for Grandma."

A wave of disappointment shot through Dwaine, and he cringed. "Am I that hard to take?"

She shook her head. "Except for our completely opposite ways of doing things, I find you attractive and fun to be with."

"I enjoy your company, too; so what's the problem?"

Sheila held up one finger. "I live in California, and you live here. Not an ideal situation for dating, wouldn't you say?"

He shrugged his shoulders. "I'm sure we can work something out."

She lifted her chin and stared at him. "Are you willing to relocate?"

"I moved from Montana to Wyoming because I like it here. I also like my antique store, and I think in time I'll make a fairly decent living because of it."

"And I have a great job in Fresno," she countered.

Dwaine opened the car door for Sheila, glad he didn't have to share the confines of his compact car with anyone else. He needed this chance to speak with Sheila alone before they headed to her grandmother's retirement center.

When he climbed into the driver's seat and clicked his door shut, Dwaine leaned toward her. "Sheila, I thought we had something going between us, and after that kiss the other night —"

She pulled away. "Can we please change the subject?"

"What do you want to talk about?"

"How about my grandmother's doll? Did you hear from the person who placed the ad in that doll magazine?"

He shook his head. "Nope. They haven't returned my call or sent any e-mails."

Her eyes clouded with obvious disappointment. "Oh."

Dwaine wanted to pull her into his arms and offer reassurance, but he figured a hug wouldn't be appreciated, and he could tell she didn't want to talk about their relationship. "If I don't hear something by tomorrow, I'll call again," he promised.

"Thanks. I appreciate that."

"This lemon chicken is delicious," Sheila said as she smiled across the table at Grandma.

Dwaine smacked his lips. "I second that, and to prove it, I'll have another piece." He stabbed a chicken leg with his fork and plopped it onto his plate.

"Sheila says you may have found my old doll," Grandma said.

He swallowed the meat he'd put in his mouth before answering. "It's a collector who buys and sells antique dolls."

"I understand there's some writing on the doll's body."

He nodded. "That's how it was stated in the description; only it didn't say what the writing said."

"I can't believe that Sheila doing something as naughty as writing her name on a doll could prove to be helpful years later." Grandma chuckled behind her napkin. "Sheila always was possessive of the doll. I never knew how much until she confessed she'd written her name on its stomach."

Dwaine laughed and shoveled another bite of meat into his mouth.

Sheila gritted her teeth. *The way these two are carrying on, you'd think I wasn't even in the room.*

"Sheila dear, you haven't said more than a few words since we sat down." Grandma wagged her finger.

"I've — uh — been eating."

"She did say she likes your chicken," Dwaine said.

"If you don't mind, I prefer to speak for myself." Sheila's voice sounded harsh, and Grandma and Dwaine looked at her like she'd taken leave of her senses.

"Are you upset about something?" Grandma asked.

Of course Sheila was upset. She'd taken a week's vacation to look for a doll Grandma had apparently sold and no one could find. Then she'd asked her boss for another two weeks so she could continue to search for the doll while helping Dwaine at his shop because he'd sprained his ankle on her account. To make matters worse, every lead they'd had so far had turned up nothing. Unless the magazine ad brought forth helpful information, it was likely Sheila would return to California without her attic treasure. Her final frustration came from falling for a guy who lived hundreds of miles from her.

"Sheila?"

"I'm fine, Grandma. Just tired, I guess."

"I'd like to date your granddaughter," Dwaine blurted, "but she's not interested."

Sheila didn't wait for Grandma's response. She leaped to her feet and raced out of the apartment.

99

Dwaine limped down the hall after Sheila, his heart pounding and his mind whirling with unanswered questions. She'd acted strangely all evening, but what had happened to set her off like this?

Dwaine caught up to Sheila as she stepped into the elevator. "Wait!"

The door started to close, but he stuck out his hand and held it open.

"Where do you think you're running off to?" he panted.

Sheila averted her gaze and stared at the floor. "Home. I'm going home."

"But you said you weren't leaving until next week."

She looked up, and her eyelids fluttered. "I'm going back to Grandma's old house, where I won't have to spend the evening being talked *about* rather than *to*."

Dwaine stepped into the elevator and pushed the button so the door would close more quickly. He didn't want to chance her bolting again.

"Ever since we sat down to supper, you and Grandma talked about me like I wasn't even in the room." Sheila's chin quivered. "I'm already upset over not finding the

Bye-Lo doll, and I don't like being treated as if I'm a child."

"I'm sorry. I didn't realize that's what I was doing."

Sheila blinked, and a few tears rolled down her cheeks. "That's not all."

"What else is bothering you?"

"I feel like all you care about is going on dates and having fun. Finding my grandmother's doll doesn't seem to be a priority anymore — if it ever was."

He shook his head. "That's not true, Sheila. I told you about the magazine ad, didn't I?"

"Yes, but what have you done to contact the person who placed it?"

"I told you before; I called and left a message on their answering machine." He sighed. "Can't really do much more until I hear back, now, can I?"

She shrugged and hung her head. "I've never run out on Grandma like that before. I don't know what came over me, and I need to go back and apologize."

"I guess it's my fault. I'm the reason you got so upset."

"No, it's my fault. I shouldn't have let myself —"

"I've enjoyed spending time with you these past few days, and I hope we can keep in touch after you return home," he interrupted.

The elevator door swished open, and Sheila hurried toward her grandmother's room. Dwaine did his best to keep up, but the pain in his ankle slowed him down.

"I'll give you my e-mail address so you can let me know what you hear on the Bye-Lo baby," she said over her shoulder.

"Right, but I was thinking more along the lines of our keeping in touch so we can build a relationship," he mumbled.

She stopped walking and turned to face him. "Again, I don't see how we can have a relationship when we live in two different states."

He gave her a sheepish grin. "Ah, that. Well, I figure if the Lord brought us together, He will make a way."

CHAPTER 10

Sheila couldn't believe her vacation was over and she was back in Fresno. Her flight had gone well, and she'd called a cab to drive her home. She should be happy and content, but instead, her heart was filled with a sense of loss that went deeper than just losing a doll. Was it possible she could love Dwaine after knowing him only a few days?

The first thing Sheila did when she stepped inside her house was check her e-mail. Sure enough, there was one from Dwaine, entitled "Response from doll collector."

As she read the message, Sheila's heart plummeted. The writing on the doll confirmed that it wasn't Grandma's. As if that wasn't bad enough news, Dwaine didn't even say he would continue to look.

"He did say he misses me," she murmured. "Guess I should be happy about that."

She glanced around the living room and loneliness crept into her soul. "I'll be okay once I'm back at work tomorrow morning. Too much vacation isn't good — especially when you return home with nothing but an ache in your heart."

Sheila wasn't sure if the pain she felt was from not finding Grandma's doll or from missing Dwaine. Probably a little of both, she decided.

"This feeling of gloom will pass. All I need to do is keep busy." She headed for the kitchen. "I'll start by cleaning the refrigerator, and then I'll go to the store and buy something good to eat. Work and food — that's what I need right now."

The next few weeks went by in a blur as Sheila immersed herself in work and tried to forget she had ever met a man named Dwaine Woods. She'd had several more e-mails from him, but he never mentioned the doll. Sheila figured either he'd had no more leads or he had no interest in trying to find the Bye-Lo for her.

"It's just as well," Sheila muttered as she turned off her work computer on Tuesday afternoon and prepared to go home.

"Were you talking to me?" Dr. Taylor

asked as he passed her desk.

Sheila felt heat creep up the back of her neck and spread quickly to her cheeks. She hadn't realized anyone else was in the room. She thought the doctor had gone home for the day.

"I didn't know you were still here."

He chuckled and pulled his fingers through the thinning gray hair at the back of his head. "If you weren't talking to me, who then?"

She stared at the blank computer screen. "Myself."

"I see. And did you have a suitable answer to your question?"

She shook her head. "I'm afraid there is no answer."

He snapped his fingers. "Sounds like a matter of the heart."

"It is," she admitted.

"Want to talk about it?"

It was tempting, for Dr. Taylor was not only an excellent chiropractor, but also a good listener, full of sound advice and godly counsel.

"It's nothing. I'll be fine," she murmured.

"All right then. I won't press the matter, but I will be praying for you."

"Thanks. I appreciate that."

"See you tomorrow morning." Dr. Taylor

grabbed his briefcase from under the front counter and headed out the door.

Sheila picked up her purse and followed.

Dwaine had closed his shop for the day, deciding to clean out the drawers of an old rolltop desk he'd discovered in a shed out behind his shop.

He gulped down the last of his coffee and pulled open the first drawer. Inside were a bunch of rubber bands, some paper clips, and a small notebook. He thumbed through the pages to be sure there was nothing important, but halted when he came to the last page.

DOLL HOSPITAL — SEATTLE was scrawled in bold letters.

"That's odd. I wonder if Bill Summers took some old dolls there to be repaired."

Dwaine thought about the box of dolls he'd acquired several weeks before. He'd been planning to take them to Seattle during Easter vacation.

"I need to get those out, because I'll be leaving for Seattle next week," Dwaine muttered as he ripped the piece of paper with the bold writing from the notebook. "Don't have a clue what this is all about, but I sure am glad for the reminder that I need to take the dolls in for repair."

He shook his head. "I think Sheila was right about me being forgetful."

Dwaine closed the drawer and stood. He hadn't heard from Sheila in a couple of days and decided to check his e-mail.

A few minutes later, he was online. There was a message from his sister, Eileen, saying they were looking forward to seeing him. There were a few e-mails from other antique shops, but nothing from Sheila. Was she too busy to write, or had she forgotten about him already?

As soon as he clicked the icon to get offline, he closed his eyes in prayer. "Father, I miss Sheila, and I really need Your help. If You want us to be together, please show me what to do."

He opened his eyes and glanced around the antique shop. Sheila had done so much to make the place look better when she was here. "I think I'd better give her a call when I get back from Seattle."

Sheila had decided a few days ago that she probably wasn't going to hear from Dwaine again. It had been over a week since she'd received an e-mail from him.

"Maybe he's given up on me because all I ever ask about is Grandma's doll and I've never said how much I miss him." She shut the computer down and pushed away from her desk. "It's probably for the best. He needs to find someone who lives there in Casper, and I need to . . ." What did she need? Sheila headed for the kitchen. "I need to fix supper and get my mind off Dwaine and the doll he's never going to find."

She chuckled in spite of her melancholy mood. She was calling dinner "supper" now. She'd been converted to Casper, Wyoming's way of saying things. Or was it Dwaine's ways she'd been converted to? Had he gotten under her skin more than she realized — carved a place in her heart she could never forget?

Sheila spotted the black Bible with worn edges — the one Dwaine had found on Grandma's old piano. Grandma had told Sheila it belonged to Grandpa and said she'd like for Sheila to have it. At the time, Sheila had thought Grandma was trying to make up for the missing doll, but now, as she stared at the cover, she was filled with a strong desire to read God's Word. She'd forgotten to do devotions that morning and knew her day would have gone better if she had done them.

She sagged into a chair and breathed a prayer. "Lord, please speak to me through Your Word, and give me a sense of peace about the things that have been troubling me since I returned home."

She opened the Bible to the book of 1 Timothy. Her gaze came to rest on chapter 6, verses 7 and 8. *"For we brought nothing into the world, and we can take nothing out of it. But if we have food and clothing, we will be content with that."*

Tears welled up in her eyes. "Father, forgive me for putting so much emphasis on worldly things. You've obviously decided I don't need Grandma's doll, and I'm realizing how wrong I've been for concentrating on a worldly possession. I should be more concerned about my relationship with You, as well as friends and family. Help me to care more, love more, and do more to further Your kingdom. Amen."

The doorbell rang, and she jumped. "It's probably the paperboy, wanting to be paid for this month's subscription."

She padded down the hall to the front door and peered through the peephole. No one was there. At least, she couldn't see anyone.

Cautiously, Sheila opened the door. Nobody was on the porch, but a small cardboard box sat on the doormat. A yellow rose lay across the top of it.

She bent down and picked them both up.

"Sure hope you like roses."

Sheila bolted upright at the sound of a deep male voice. A voice she recognized and had longed to hear. "Dwaine?"

He peeked around the corner of the house and grinned at her.

"Wh–what are you doing here?" she rasped.

"Came to see you."

"What about the rose and package? What are they for?"

He stepped onto the porch. "The rose is to say, 'I've missed you,' and what's in the box is a gift from my heart."

She looked at the package, at Dwaine, and back at the package again. "What's in there?"

"Open it and find out."

Sheila handed him the rose and lifted the lid. She gasped, and her eyes clouded with tears as a Bye-Lo baby came into view. The skin on her arms turned to gooseflesh. Could it possibly be Grandma's old doll?

With trembling fingers and a galloping heart, Sheila raised the cotton nightgown. It was there — her name scrawled in black ink on the cloth stomach.

She clutched the Bye-Lo baby to her chest. "Oh Dwaine, where did you find her?"

"In Seattle. It's an interesting story. Can I step inside out of this heat?" Dwaine wiped the perspiration from his forehead.

"Yes, of course. Come in and I'll pour you some iced tea."

When they were both seated at the kitchen table with glasses of cold tea, Sheila said, "Don't keep me in suspense. Please tell me how all this came about."

Dwaine set down his glass and grinned. "It was an answer to prayer."

"Going to Seattle, finding the doll, or coming here?"

"All three." He leaned closer and she shivered, even though she wasn't cold.

His lips were inches from hers, and she could feel his warm breath against her face. Mustering all her willpower, Sheila leaned away. "H–how much do I owe you for the doll?"

"What?" Dwaine looked dazed.

"Bye-Lo. How much did she cost?"

"Nothing."

"Nothing?"

He shook his head. "Let me explain."

"Please do."

"Last week I was cleaning out an old desk I had found in the shed behind my shop, and I came across a notebook. One of the pages had the words 'Doll Hospital —

Seattle,' written on it."

"That's all?"

"Yep. I had no idea what it meant, but it reminded me that I had a box of old dolls I wanted to take there." Dwaine paused to take another sip of tea. "After spending Easter with my sister and her family in Seattle, I went to the doll hospital the following day."

"That's where you found my grandmother's doll?"

He nodded. "As soon as I told the lady where I was from and that I was the new owner of The Older the Better Antique Shop, she lit right up. Said a Bye-Lo doll had been sent from the previous owner several months ago and that she'd never heard back from him."

"I'm surprised she didn't call the store."

"She said she'd tried but was told the number had been disconnected. Turns out she'd been given a wrong number." Dwaine set his glass back on the table. "Since she knew the number she'd called wasn't in service, she assumed the business had closed."

"So she kept the doll?"

"Right. She put in new eyes, since that's what it had been sent there for, and placed the doll in her display cabinet. Said she didn't want to sell the Bye-Lo in case the man who sent it ever tried to contact her."

Sheila stared at the doll lying on the table. Its pale pink bisque face looked as sweet as it had when she was a child. "You didn't have to buy it, then?"

"Nope. Just paid the woman the bill to fix the eyes."

"But what about the amount my grand-mother was paid by the previous owner of your shop?"

Dwaine shrugged. "Don't know how much that was since I can't find a receipt."

"I'm sure Grandma knows what she sold it for."

He shook his head. "I called and asked, but she said she forgot."

"At least let me pay for the cost of the doll's repairs and your plane ticket to bring it to me." Sheila smiled. "You could have saved yourself the trouble and mailed it, you know."

He squinted and shook his head. "And miss the chance to see you?"

She squirmed in her chair as his expression grew more intense.

"I've missed you, Sheila. Missed your laughing eyes, beautiful smile, and even your organizational skills." He leaned closer. "I believe I've fallen in love with you."

Her mouth went dry. "You — you have?"

He nodded and lifted her chin with his thumb. "I know we haven't known each other very long, but when God brings a good thing into my life, I'd be a fool to ignore it."

"I agree."

His eyes twinkled. "You think I'm a good thing?"

"Oh yes," she murmured. "God's been showing me some important verses from His Word, and as happy as I am to have the precious Bye-Lo baby, I'm even more excited to see you."

As Dwaine's lips sought hers, Sheila felt like she was floating on a cloud. When the kiss ended, they both spoke at once.

"Does Fresno need another antique shop?"

"Does Casper need another chiropractor's receptionist?"

They laughed.

"I could use a secretary. As you already know, my shop was a mess before you came along." Dwaine took hold of her hand and gave it a gentle squeeze. "And I've been a mess since you left town."

"Me, too." Sheila smiled through her tears. "I've been doing a lot of thinking lately, and I've decided there's really nothing keeping me here in Fresno. I know, too, that building a relationship with someone as wonderful as you is far more important than my job or the old doll I used to play with as a child."

"You mean it?" He sounded hopeful, and his eyes searched her face. "What about your parents' house? Would you sell this place if you moved to Casper?"

She shook her head. "Just a minor detail. The house can be put up for rent."

His lips touched her forehead in a kiss as gentle as the flicker of butterfly wings. "I know it's probably too soon for a marriage proposal, but if you move to Casper, we can work on that."

She fingered the cloth body on the Bye-Lo baby. "And to think none of this would have happened if I hadn't come to Wyoming in search of Grandma's doll."

ABOUT THE AUTHOR

Wanda E. Brunstetter is a bestselling author who enjoys writing Amish-themed as well as contemporary and historical novels. Descended from Anabaptists herself, Wanda became deeply interested in the Plain People when she married her husband, Richard, who grew up in a Mennonite church in Pennsylvania. Wanda and her husband live in Washington State but take every opportunity to visit their Amish friends in various communities across the country, gathering further information about the Amish way of life.

Wanda and her husband have two grown children and six grandchildren. In her spare time, Wanda enjoys photography, ventriloquism, gardening, reading, stamping, and having fun with her family.

In addition to her novels, Wanda has written Amish cookbooks, Amish devotionals, and several Amish children's books as well as numerous novellas, stories, articles, poems, and puppet scripts.

Visit Wanda's website at www.wandabrunstetter.com and feel free to e-mail her at wanda@wandabrunstetter.com.

The employees of Thorndike Press hope you have enjoyed this Large Print book. All our Thorndike, Wheeler, and Kennebec Large Print titles are designed for easy reading, and all our books are made to last. Other Thorndike Press Large Print books are available at your library, through selected bookstores, or directly from us.

For information about titles, please call:
(800) 223-1244

or visit our Web site at:
http://gale.cengage.com/thorndike

To share your comments, please write:
Publisher
Thorndike Press
10 Water St., Suite 310
Waterville, ME 04901